Jackie Laroo
boy pirate
A Pirates Lesson

Written by Jay Annis

Illustrations by Jerry Goff

ISBN: 978-0-9854584-0-9
Printed by Theo Davis Printing, Inc., Zebulon, NC

To my little ladies,
it was you and only you,
who gave the world Mr. Jackie Laroo!
J.A.

Before there was Blackbeard and pirates of the like, there lived the most incredible famous young tike. He became a pirate at the earliest age, and this is the first time his story has been penned to a page. I know you are thinking who is he? Who? Who? He goes by the name of Jackie LaRoo.

You see being a pirate is somewhat of an art,
and here's how Jackie LaRoo got his start
Well, his mom loved the sea, had a boat named
Kazoo, and his dad was a whaler in year twenty tu
It ran in their blood which ran into his, so it was
only right that Jackie ended up in the biz.

It started before birth, if you must know.
In his mom's belly he would put on a show.
He made a big fuss while cooking inside,
tossing and turning with the flow of the tide.
Up and down he would glide as if riding on air.
Dreams of ships and high seas his only care.

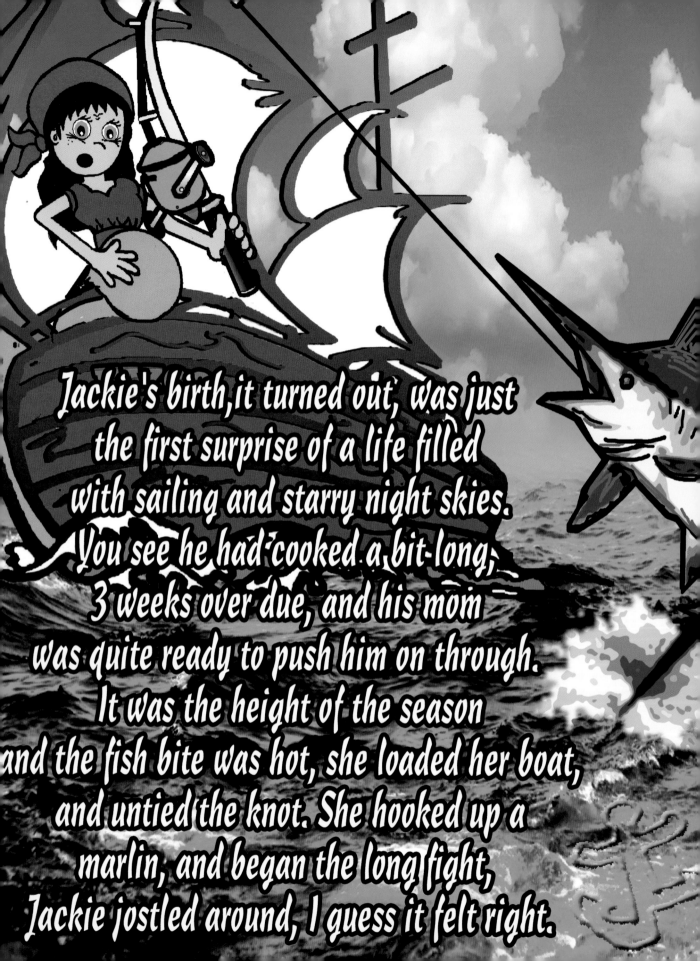

Jackie's birth, it turned out, was just
the first surprise of a life filled
with sailing and starry night skies.
You see he had cooked a bit long,
3 weeks over due, and his mom
was quite ready to push him on through.
It was the height of the season
and the fish bite was hot, she loaded her boat,
and untied the knot. She hooked up a
marlin, and began the long fight,
Jackie jostled around, I guess it felt right.

Jackie was born with one eye and only one leg, but they fixed him right up with a patch and a peg. His first gift was a parrot fresh from the nest, they decked him all out with a hat and a vest. With no rhyme or reason he was named Tuffins McGee, the bird was hooked to Jackie like Jackie to the sea.

At two he had already accomplished more than most, he sailed round the islands and down the crystal coast. He grew up fast, oh! he did thrive, had a schooner named Seafus, at only age five. It got lonely at sea with only the two, so he pulled into port and captained a crew.

The men were quite wary
at first sight of the cap 'n ,
but fell into line
when Jackie
began snappin'.
They pulled up
the anchor and
fastened the mast,
the folks on shore
just stared
as they passed.

Jackie met royalty when he was just eight. Chris Columbus it was, who said his directions were great. He quickly became known from shore to shore, and there wasn't a pirate alive who wouldn't carry his oar.

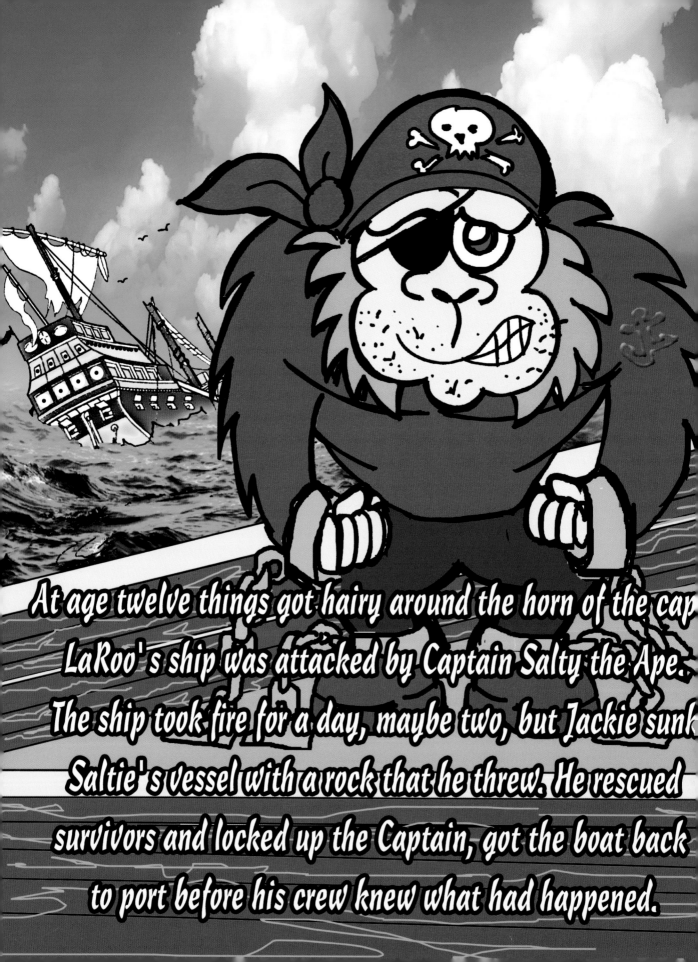

At age twelve things got hairy around the horn of the cap LaRoo's ship was attacked by Captain Salty the Ape. The ship took fire for a day, maybe two, but Jackie sunk Saltie's vessel with a rock that he threw. He rescued survivors and locked up the Captain, got the boat back to port before his crew knew what had happened.

time went by Jackie had urges to hunt treasure, and would
pture his booty no matter the measure. He rescued a chest filled
th pure Spanish gold, which was guarded by dragons,
legend was told. LaRoo picked up a necklace
m a mermaid named Bliss,
o gave it to Jackie
en he promised a kiss.
e had coins and chains and jewels of the
e, he would capture his prize
matter the hike.

As time went by Jackie began to feel a weird pain. It started in his toes, then went to his brain. The doctors were puzzled, they didn't know where to start, and before long the pain went straight to his heart.

Jackie talked to gypsies, the witches, the sailors,
He talked with the banker, the sheriff and jailers.
Not a one of em' knew about a possible cure,
so he headed down to port feeling very unsure.
Just when he thought he had lost all his will,
he saw an old man sitting just down the hill.
As Jackie passed by he looked at the man,
who stood and faced Jackie and stuck out his hand.

He said the names Elmore, I know who you are,
your Jackie Laroo, and your a big star.
Iv'e heard all the stories and read all the papers
about the wild escapes and all your daring caper
There's just one big problem your hurting inside,
its really quite clear when I look in your eyes.

Jackie was nervous, and he began to sweat.
e was sure his disease would get the best of him yet.
The man calmly placed his hand over Jackie's heart,
and said here is your problem your falling apart.
Your heart is all hollow, with nothing inside,
no love, no laughter, only dumb pride.

You see Jackie had not been home in 12 years,
no family, no love, and no happy tears.
On his quest for adventure he lost sight of the thing
that make people whole and give children wings.
He needed the love of his mom and his pop,
and without them close by the pain would not stop.

The man gazed straight at Jackie,
and said "listen here son".
"Get on that ship and make the long run.
Back to your home, to your mom and your dad",
the advice was the best,
better than any Jackie had had.

He arrived back home in a couple of weeks,
navigating the rivers, the shoals and the creeks.
His mom was right there in the kitchen cooking dinner,
and the moment he saw her he felt more like a winner.
They hugged and he cried, and she said its all right,
we're here for you Jackie in the day or the night.

Jackie learned something very important that day.
That treasure and fame aren't all that they say.
You can stack it all up, as high as the sky,
but it doesn't come close to what money
can't buy. The love and support
of family is key, even to
a boy who's king
of the sea.